SHORT TALES

GREEK MYTHS

ARACHNE

Adapted by J.J. Hart
Illustrated by Cynthia Martin

GREEN LEVEL	BLUE LEVEL	PINK LEVEL
• Familiar topics	• New ideas introduced	• More complex ideas
• Frequently used words	• Larger vocabulary	• Extended vocabulary
• Repeating language patterns	• Variety of language patterns	• Expanded sentence structures

To learn more about Short Tales leveling, go to www.abdopublishing.com

Published by Magic Wagon, a division of the ABDO Publishing Group, 8000 West 78th Street, Edina, Minnesota 55439. Copyright © 2008 by Abdo Consulting Group, Inc. International copyrights reserved in all countries. All rights reserved. No part of this book may be reproduced in any form without written permission from the publisher. Short Tales ™ is a trademark and logo of Magic Wagon.

Printed in the United States.

Adapted text by J.J. Hart
Illustrations by Cynthia Martin
Colors by Wes Hartman
Edited by Stephanie Hedlund
Interior Layout by Kristen Fitzner Denton
Book Design and Packaging by Shannon Eric Denton

Library of Congress Cataloging-in-Publication Data

Hart, J. J.
 Arachne / adapted by J. J. Hart ; illustrated by Cynthia Martin.
   p. cm. -- (Short tales. Greek myths)
 ISBN 978-1-60270-134-2
 1. Arachne (Greek mythology)--Juvenile literature. I. Martin, Cynthia. II. Title.

BL820.A75H37 2008
398.20938'02--dc22

                          2007036066

THE GREEK GODS

ZEUS:
Ruler of Gods
& Men

ATHENA:
Goddess of
Wisdom

HEPHAESTUS:
God of Fire
& Metalworking

HERA:
Goddess of Marriage
Queen of the Gods

HERMES:
Messenger of
the Gods

HESTIA:
Goddess of the
Hearth & Home

POSEIDON:
God of the Sea

APHRODITE:
Goddess of Love

ARES:
God of War

ARTEMIS:
Goddess of
the Hunt

APOLLO:
God of the Sun

HADES:
God of the
Underworld

Mythical Beginning

The goddess Athena sprang full-grown from the head of Zeus, wearing full armor. She defended Athens, protected civilization, and looked after agriculture and handicrafts. In this role, she was a skilled seamstress and weaver. Her temple was the Parthenon. She is said to have invented the bridle, allowing humans to tame and ride horses.

As with most of the gods and goddesses, Athena was proud of the things she could do. She didn't take lightly the claims of mere mortals that they could do as well.

Arachne was a young peasant woman from a small village. She had incredible skill with her loom. The compliments of those around her swelled her head with pride.

She believed so completely in her own abilities that she was willing to compare them to anyone's, even the goddess Athena's.

Once, a peasant woman named Arachne lived in a small village.

Everyone in town marveled at her weaving skill.

Even the nymphs came from the woods to enjoy the things she made.

Sometimes people gathered around to watch her work.

They liked seeing the spools of yarn turn into colorful pictures on her loom.

One day a woman said, "Your work is so stunning. Athena herself must have taught you."

Proud Arachne grew angry.

"No one taught me," she said. "I learned all on my own. No one is a better weaver than I, not even a goddess."

"If Athena thinks she is better than me, let her prove it," Arachne said.

The people gasped in fear.

No one challenged the gods this way!

Athena was the goddess of wisdom.

She also loved to spin and weave.

Her beautiful weavings showed the gods and goddesses of Mount Olympus.

No mortal being could hope to make such lovely things.

The gods and goddesses knew when people were talking about them.

When Athena heard Arachne compare her skills to Athena's, she grew furious.

"How dare she?" Athena cried.

Athena disguised herself as an old woman and left Mount Olympus.

Soon she came to Arachne's village.

When she met Arachne, she was friendly.

"Your weaving is very fine," she said. "But you should not mock Athena. If you ask her to forgive you, I'm sure she will show you mercy. She is very kind and wise."

Arachne would not apologize.

"I am not afraid of her," she said. "If Athena thinks she weaves better than I do, let her prove it."

"Very well," Athena said, showing her true self. "I will prove it."

All the townsfolk and the nymphs bowed before the goddess.

"We will have a contest," Athena said. Arachne remained standing.

Only her blushing cheeks showed that she was at all frightened.

She agreed to Athena's contest.

Athena and Arachne sat at their looms and began weaving.

They fed in wools and threads of every color.

They used blues and reds, greens and yellows, and black and white. They even included silver, gold, and copper.

As she wove, Arachne began to worry.

She believed in herself. But, she was a mortal woman, competing with a goddess!

What if she failed?

The colors blended on Arachne's loom, like paint on a canvas.

Arachne added some yellow to make brown tree trunks and the sides of mountains.

768

Athena's weaving showed a contest she had once had with Poseidon, ruler of the sea.

Around this were scenes of the gods overcoming humans in different ways.

She hoped this would warn
Arachne to beware of competing
against a goddess.

Arachne's picture showed times gods
had made mistakes in their dealings
with mortals.

Her weaving was every bit as beautiful
as Athena's.

Both weavers finished at the same moment.

Athena looked at Arachne's weaving.

Seeing Arachne's work made Athena even angrier.

Arachne had proven that her skills were the equal of a goddess's.

But her picture was an insult.

In her fury, Athena cut the web that Arachne had woven.

Then Athena touched Arachne gently on the forehead.

When she did, Arachne felt ashamed that she had been so full of pride.

Arachne was confused and
embarrassed.

She didn't know what else to do.

She hurried to a nearby tree and
hung herself.

When Athena saw what Arachne had done, she felt sorry for her.

Arachne was a brave woman to challenge a goddess.

Athena went to Arachne and helped her to live.

But, Athena didn't want Arachne to forget how foolish she had been.

So, she sprinkled Arachne with a magic potion.

Arachne awoke and began to change.

The potion turned Arachne into a spider.

In this form, she would always be able to spin the most beautiful webs.

She passed this gift on to her children.

Arachne was no longer human.

So, Athena would always be able to say that no human could weave as well as her.